S0-AFQ-910

TINY TROLL TREASURY
THE LITTLEST TROLL

Illustrated by
Joe Veno

Publications International, Ltd.

Teeny Troll stood as straight and tall as she could. Perhaps this time the other troll boys and girls would pick her for their team.

One by one, the captains took turns choosing their team members until only Teeny was left. "You can't play acorn-toss with us, Teeny. You're too little. Why don't you go hunt for ladybugs or something," they said.

Teeny wiped away a tear and walked home, where she found her mother in bed with the blanket pulled up to her chin. "Are you sick, Mama?" asked Teeny.

"I have a cold," said her mother. "I need some rest."

Teeny had a wonderful idea. She would make lunch for her mother and bring it to her in bed. She set to work making dandelion soup, cornflower muffins, and iced frostberry juice.

Cooking wasn't easy. First, the bag of cornflower flour spilled. Then the frostberry juice tipped over and leaked onto the floor. And with a crash, all the pots and pans toppled out of the cupboard.

"What is going on in here?" cried Teeny's mother from the kitchen doorway. "Look at this mess!"

"I wanted to help by fixing lunch," said Teeny. "I guess I'm too small."

*T*eeny decided to watch her father paint their house. He was painting a spot high on the front porch. Teeny knew he wouldn't be able to reach his bucket of paint. "Let me help, Papa," she said. She picked up the paint bucket to carry it closer to him.

"No, Teeny! You're too little for that heavy bucket of…," warned her father. It was too late. Teeny's father was wearing a fresh coat of paint from head to toe!

After she and her father cleaned up the paint, Teeny took a fishing pole down to the stream. "At least this is something I can't mess up," she said to herself.

She settled on the soft grassy bank and dropped her hook in the water. She felt a nibble and then SPLASH! Teeny was sitting in the middle of the stream!

The fish were laughing at Teeny as if to say, "You are too little to catch a fish!"

*T*eeny wept, "I'm too little for everything. Nobody needs a little troll like me." Just then, the trolls from the village ran past her. They had worried looks on their faces.

"Hurry!" they cried.

"What's wrong?" asked Teeny as she joined them.

"It's baby Dewdrop!" answered Teeny's father. "She has crawled into a hollow tree and she can't get out!"

When everyone arrived at the hollow tree, they saw a very small opening and heard the frightened cry of baby Dewdrop.

Dewdrop's mother and father wrung their hands in despair. "We've tried everything, but we can't get her out. We're all too big to fit through the hole. What will we do?"

While everyone stood around talking about plans to reach Dewdrop, Teeny Troll had an idea of her own!

Teeny peered into the hole in the hollow tree. "This isn't such a small hole—it's just my size!" she thought. Teeny slipped through the hole and reached Dewdrop in no time.

"Come on, Dewdrop. I'll get you out of here." The baby smiled and let Teeny carry her out of the scary, dark hollow tree.

"Teeny saved Dewdrop!" cried the relieved trolls when they saw her holding Dewdrop. "Teeny saved the day!"

*T*eeny was a happy little troll as she rode home on her father's proud shoulders.

"Teeny," said her mother, "You may be little in size, but you were a very big girl today!"

And do you know, the other troll children must have thought so, too. The next day, they picked her *first* for their acorn-toss team!